# Ocean Swell

By Richenda Court

Published by Richenda Court 2016
**www. richendacourt.co.uk**

Illustrations © Richenda Court 2016

All rights reserved.
No part of this publication can be reproduced, stored in or introduced to a retrieval system, or transmitted in any form or by any means (electronic, mechanical, photocopying, recording or otherwise) without the prior written permission of the publisher. Requests for permission should be sent to richenda@richendacourt.co.uk.

A CIP catalogue record of this book is available from the British Library.

ISBN 978-1-5262-0586-5

Book designed and typeset by Openhouse Creative.
**www.openhousecreative.co.uk**

This book was successfully funded by a Kickstarter campaign.
**www.kickstarter.com**

Printed and bound in Hersham, Surrey
by Impress Print.

| SURREY LIBRARIES | |
|---|---|
| | |
| Askews & Holts | 14-Jun-2017 |
| GRB | £12.99 |
| | |

To Simon, Curtis & Hermione

*'...whenever he passed, her words returned sparkling.'*

Disenchanted with the real world in an English seaside town, The Boy and The Girl immerse themselves in the ocean for an underwater journey. The dreams of The Boy and The Girl, carried within star urchins, are known by soul keepers who patiently watch over them from tiny wooden boats as they begin to re-discover hope and optimism.

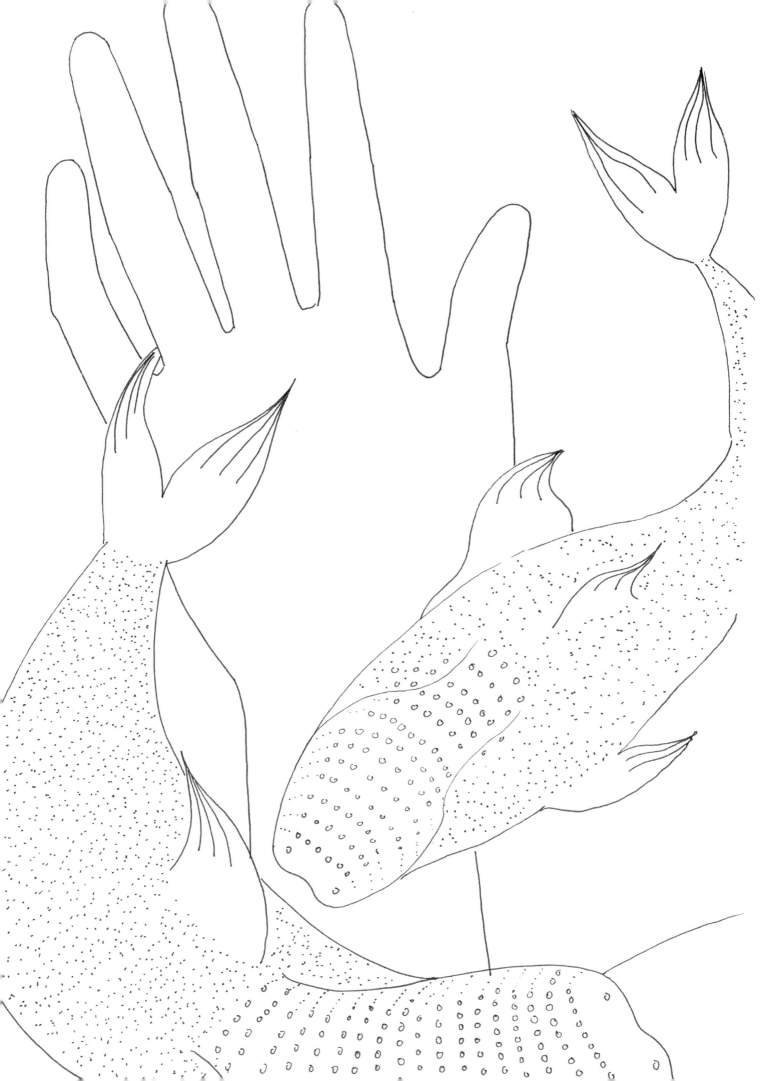

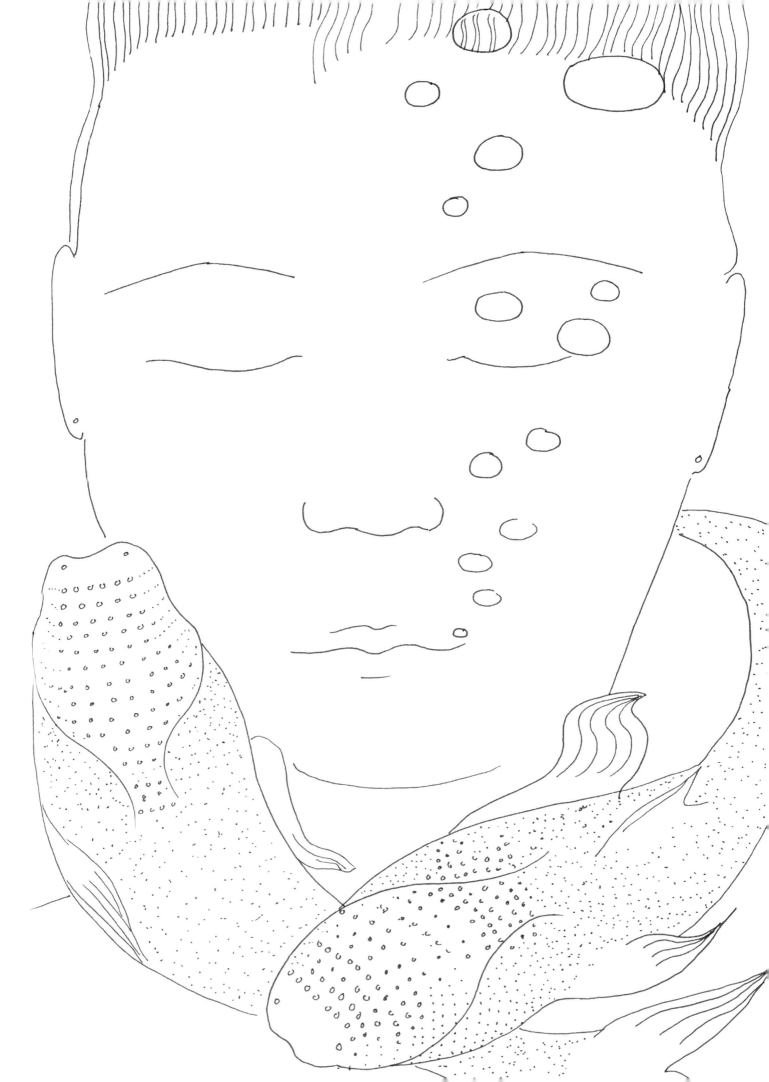

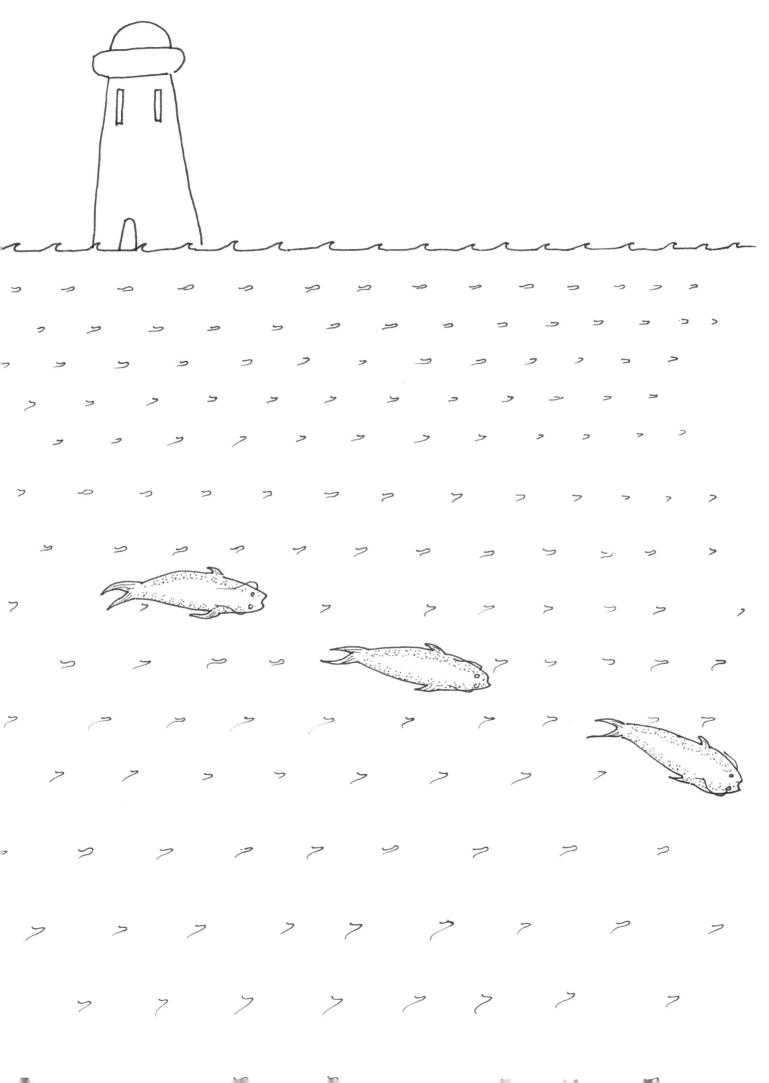

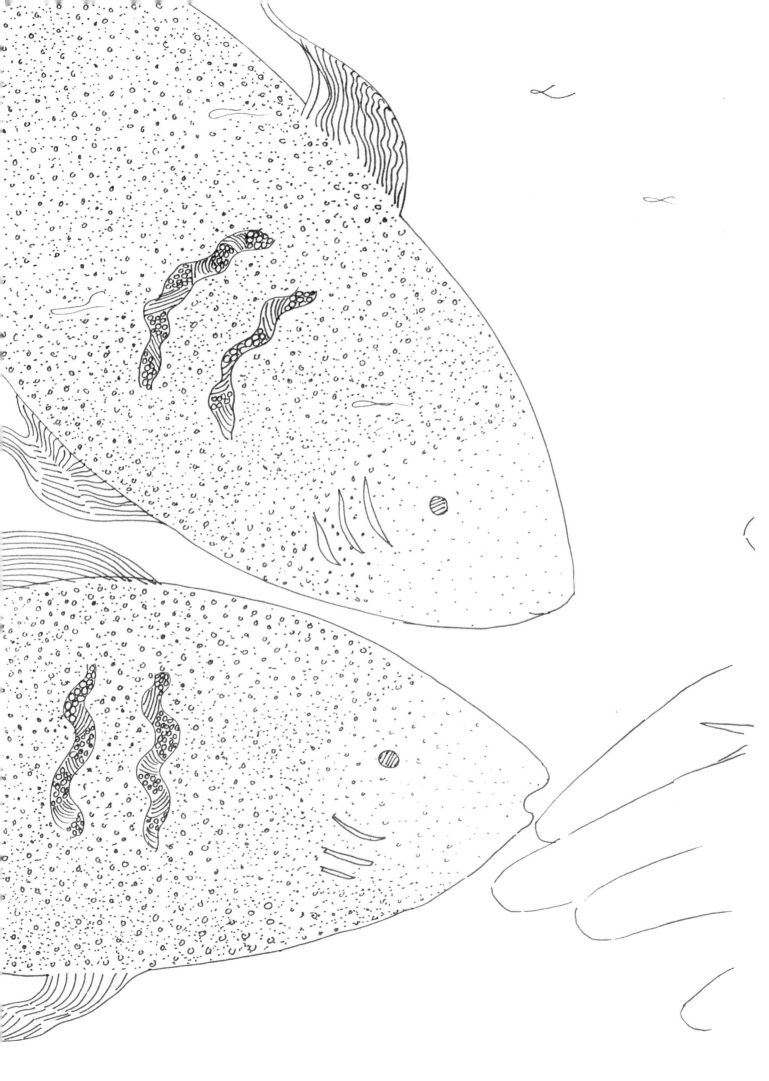

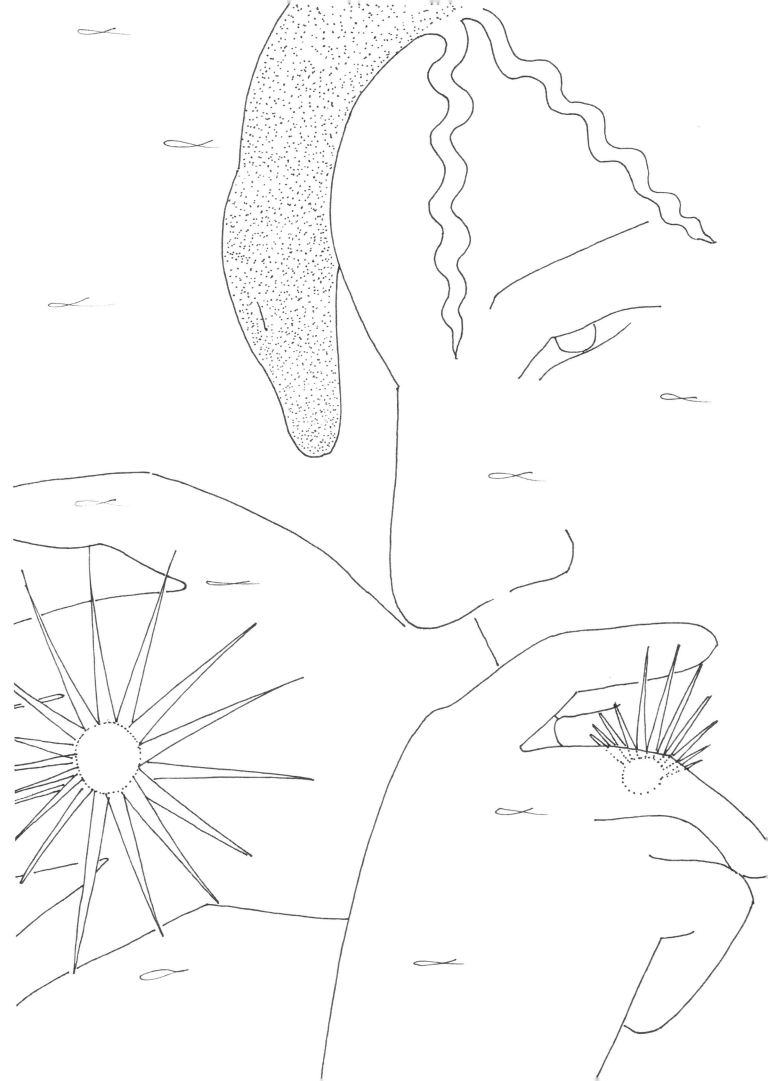

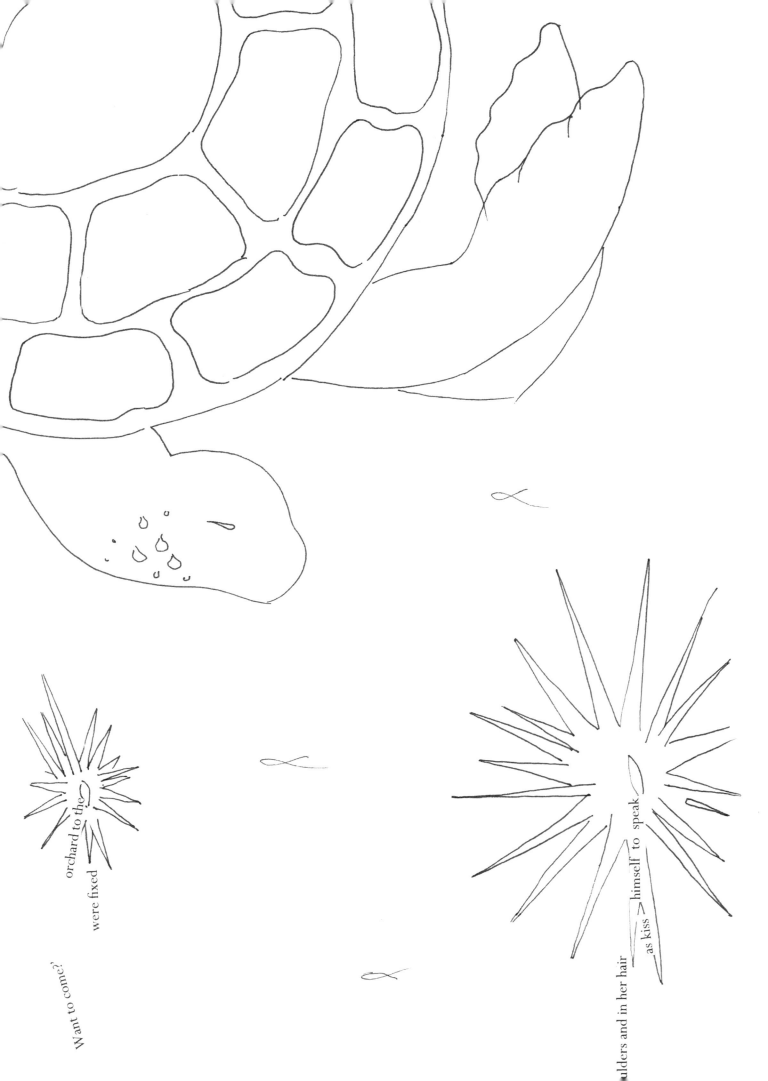

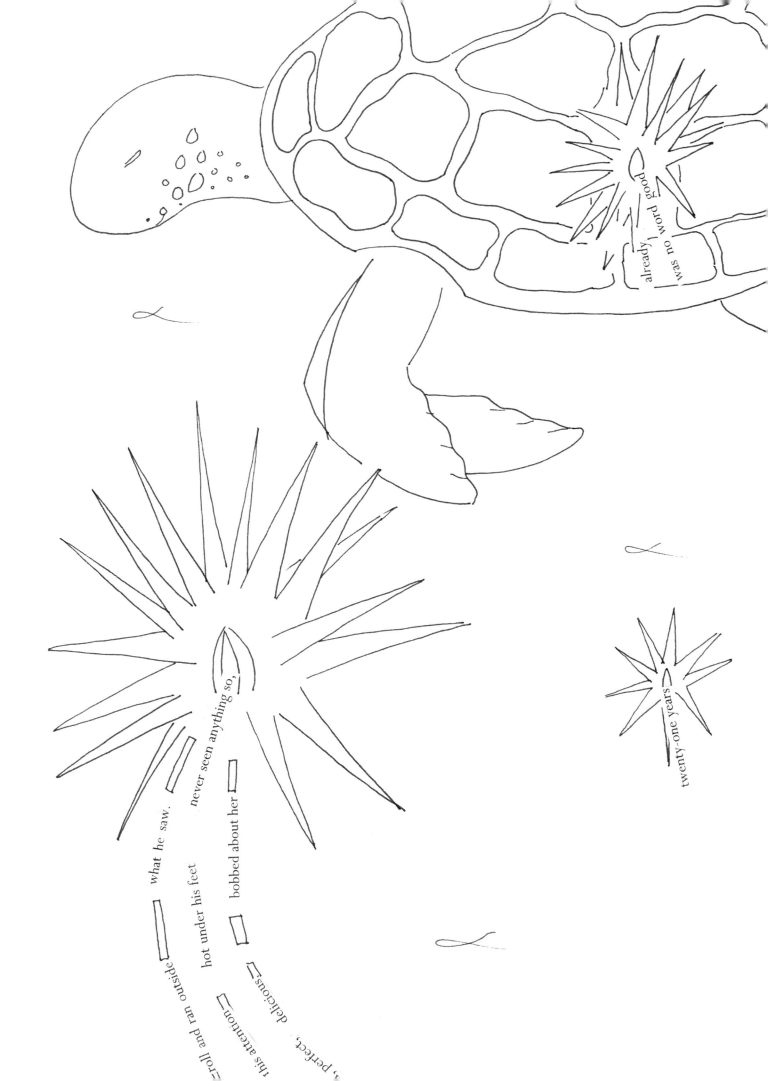

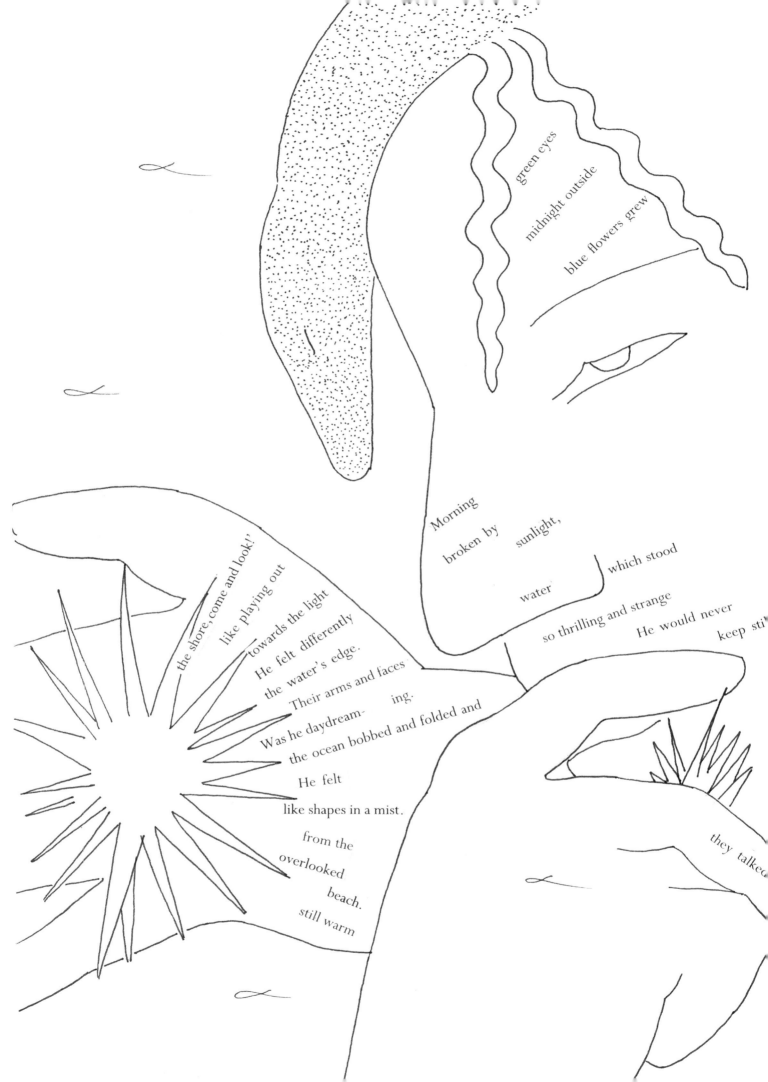

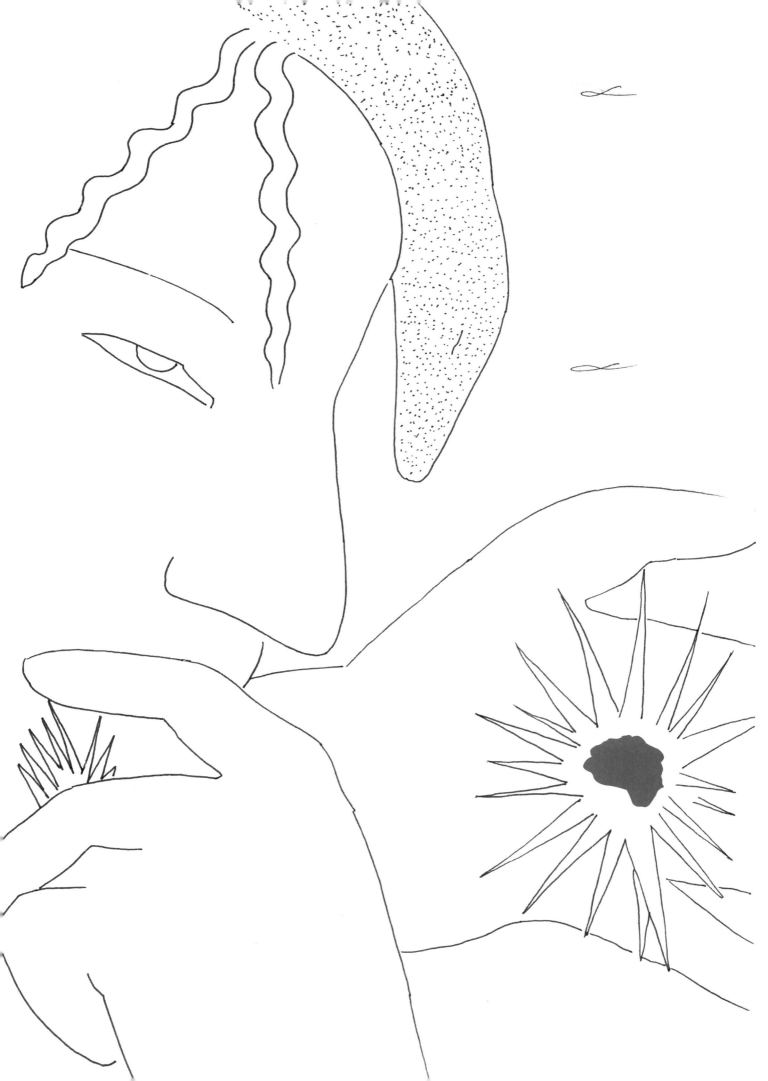

his eyes closed,

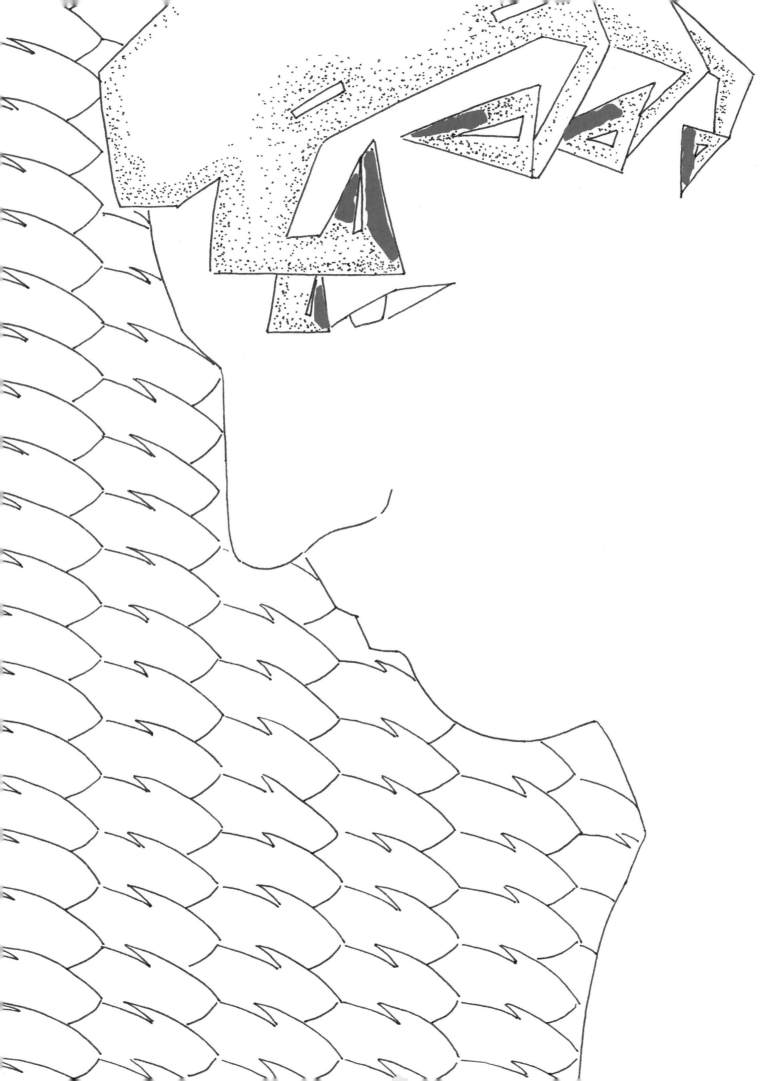

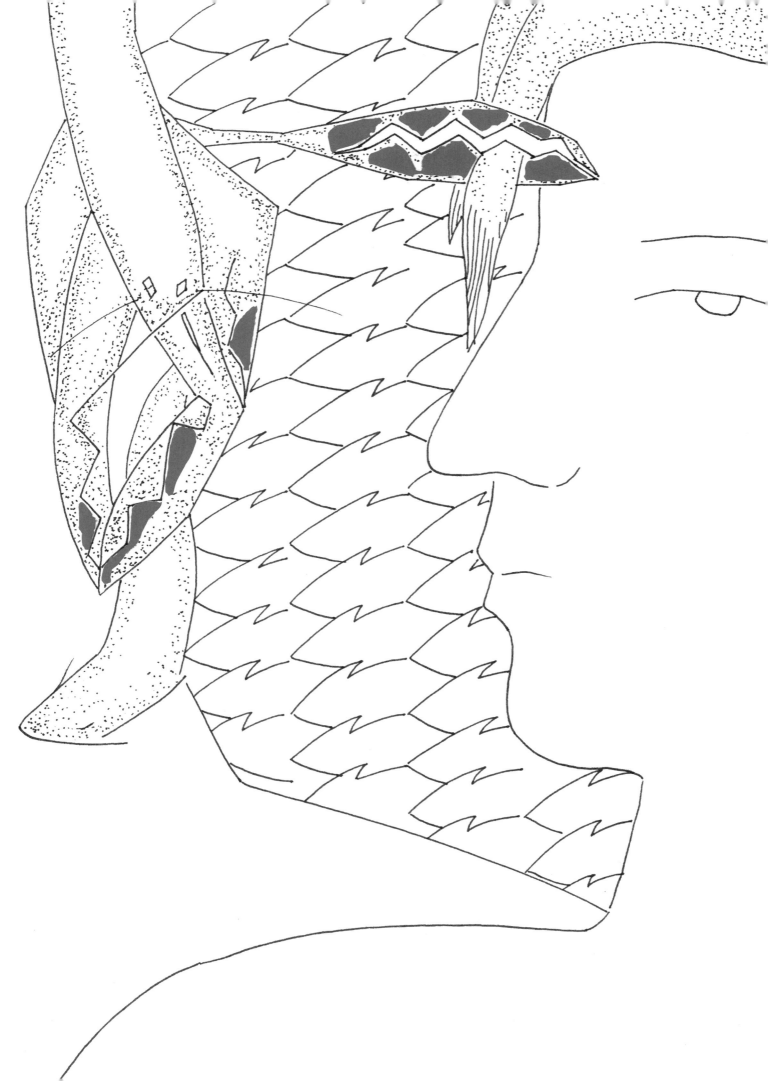

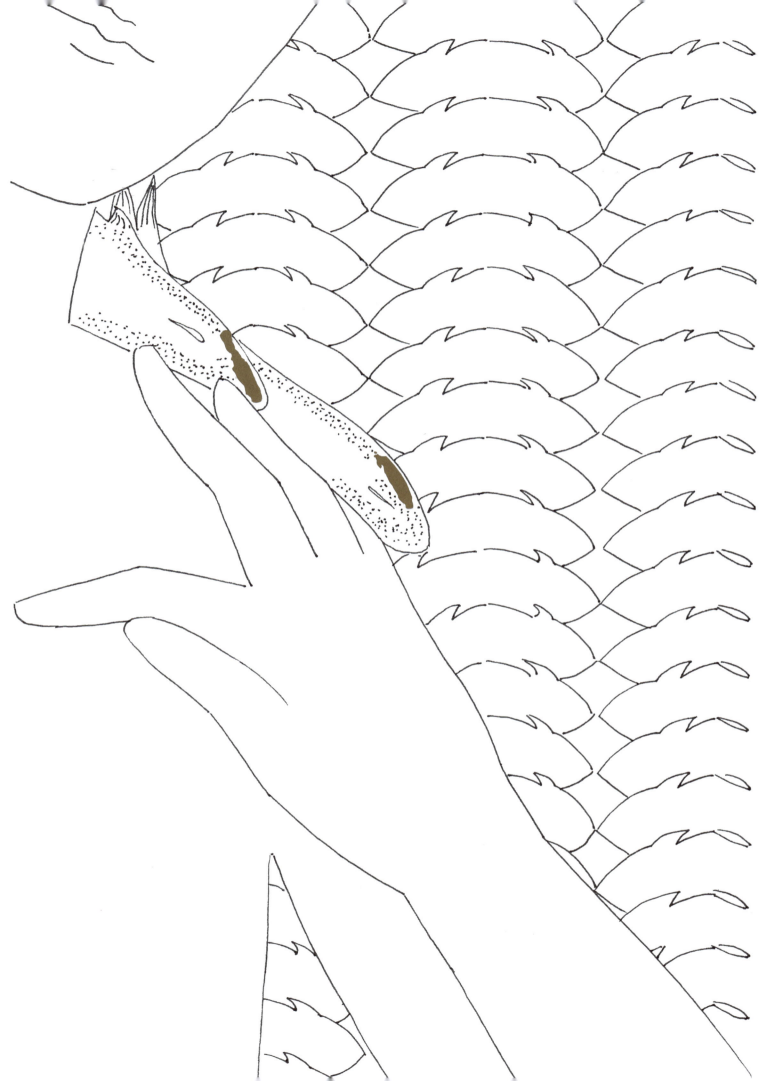

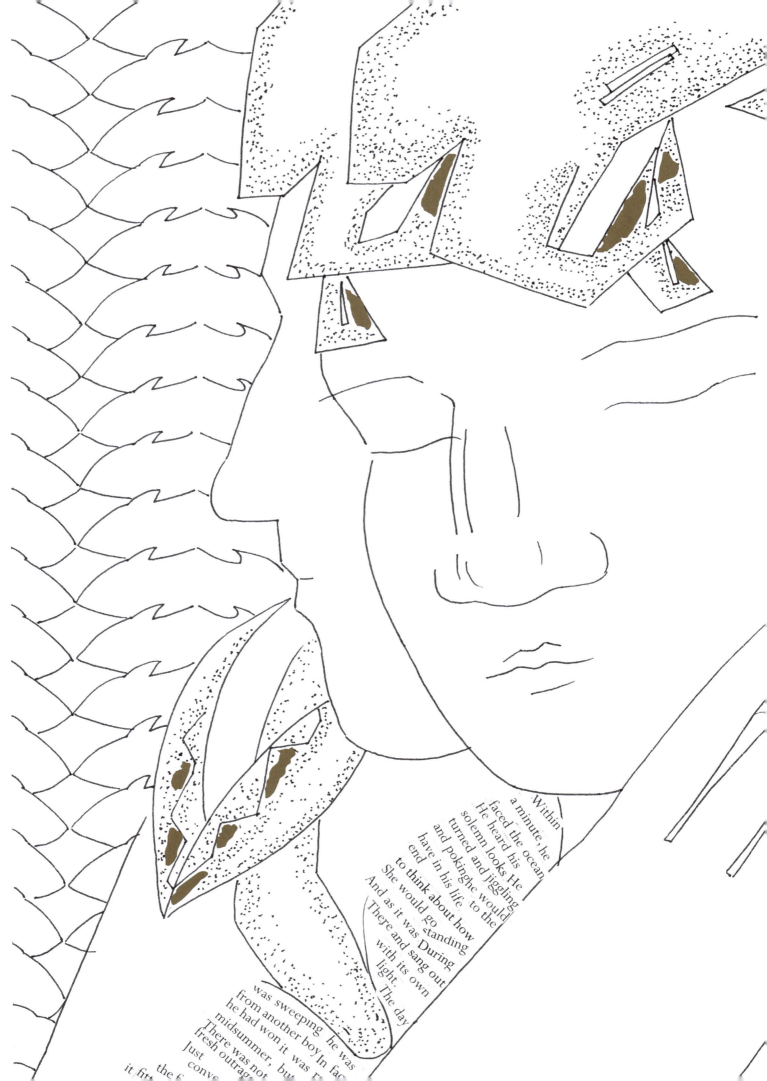

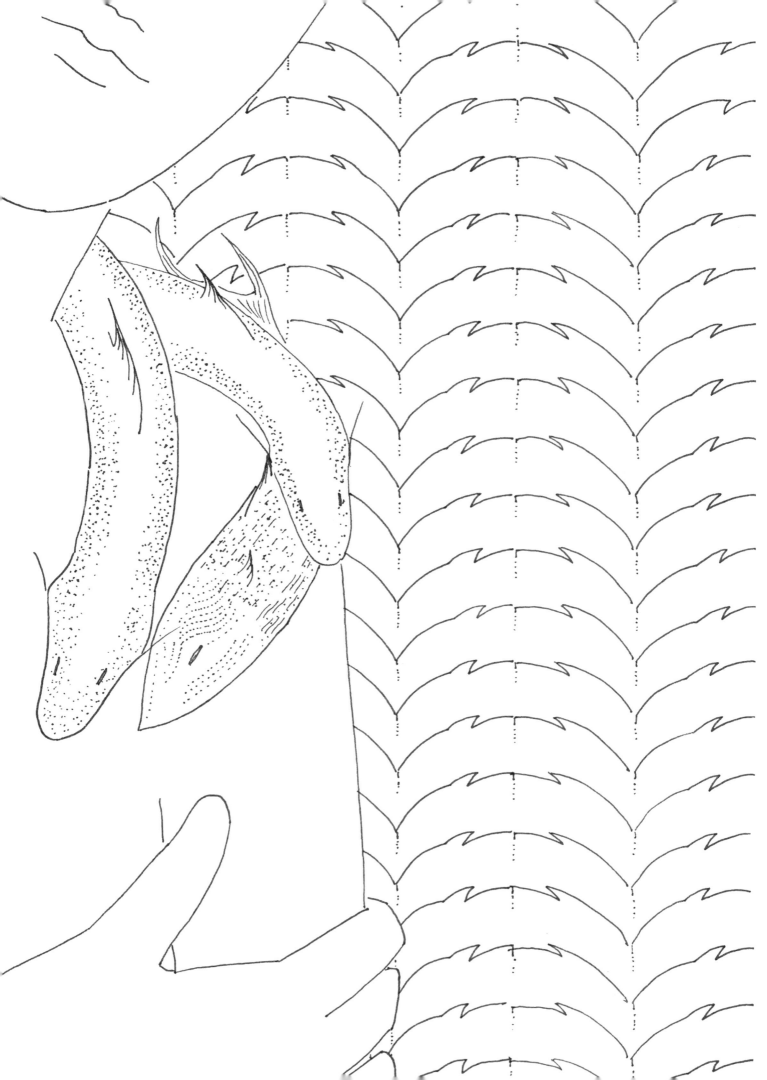

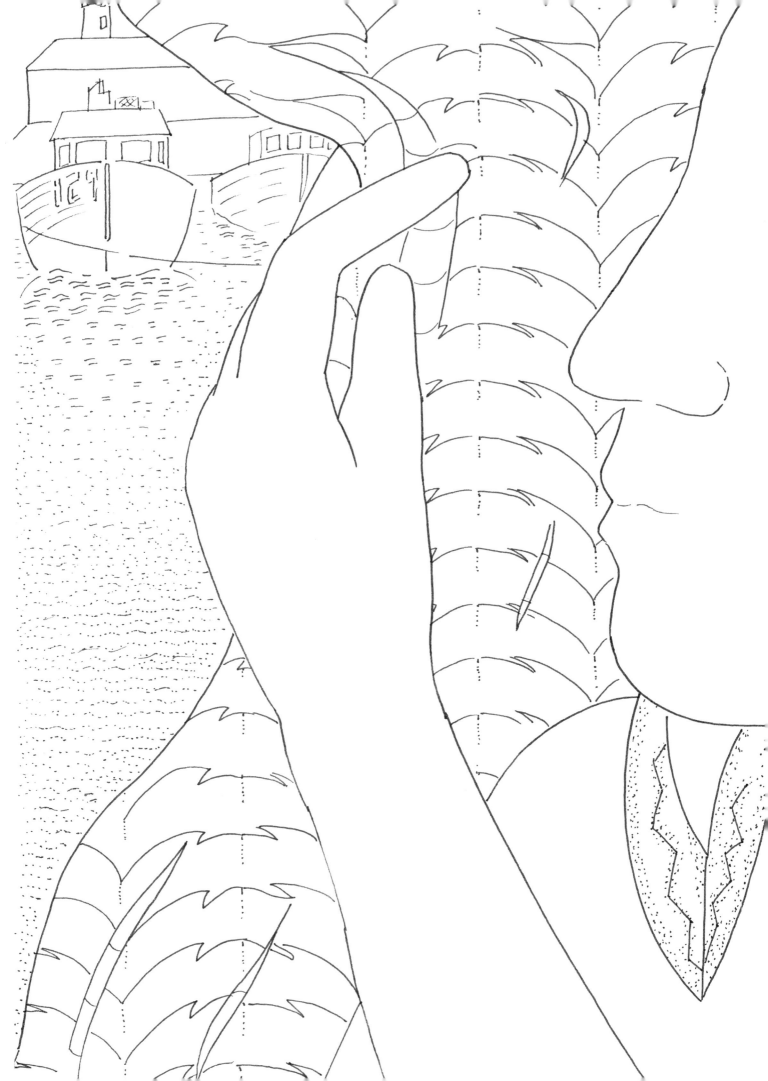

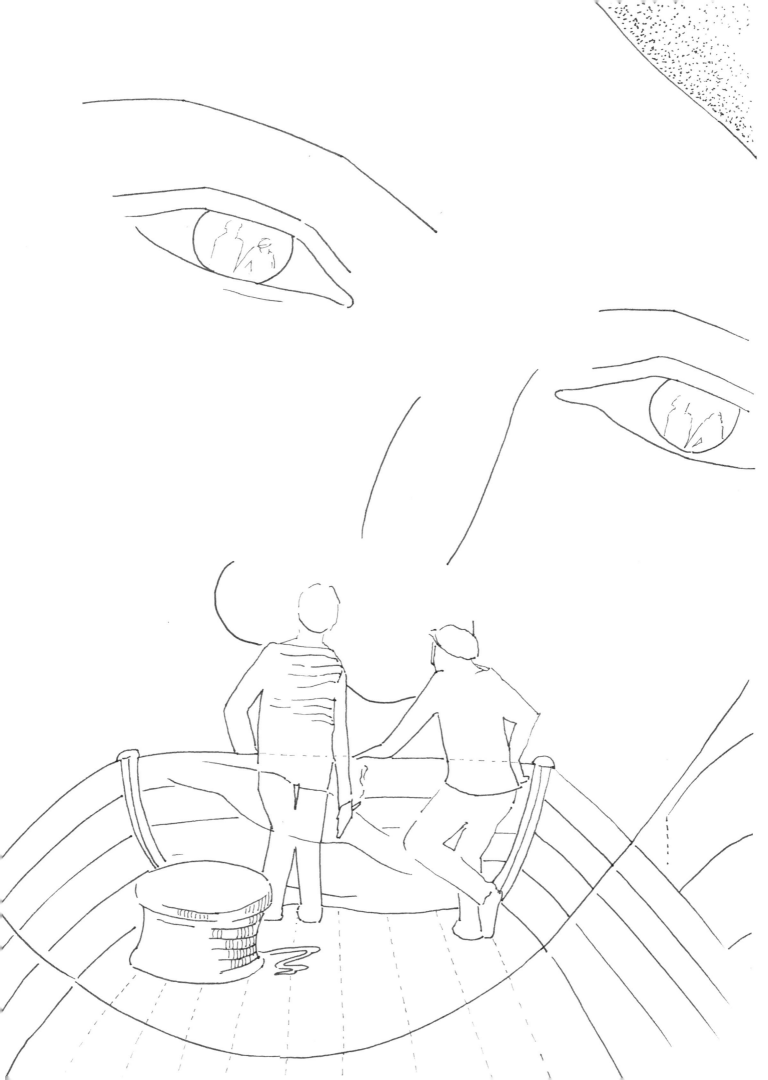

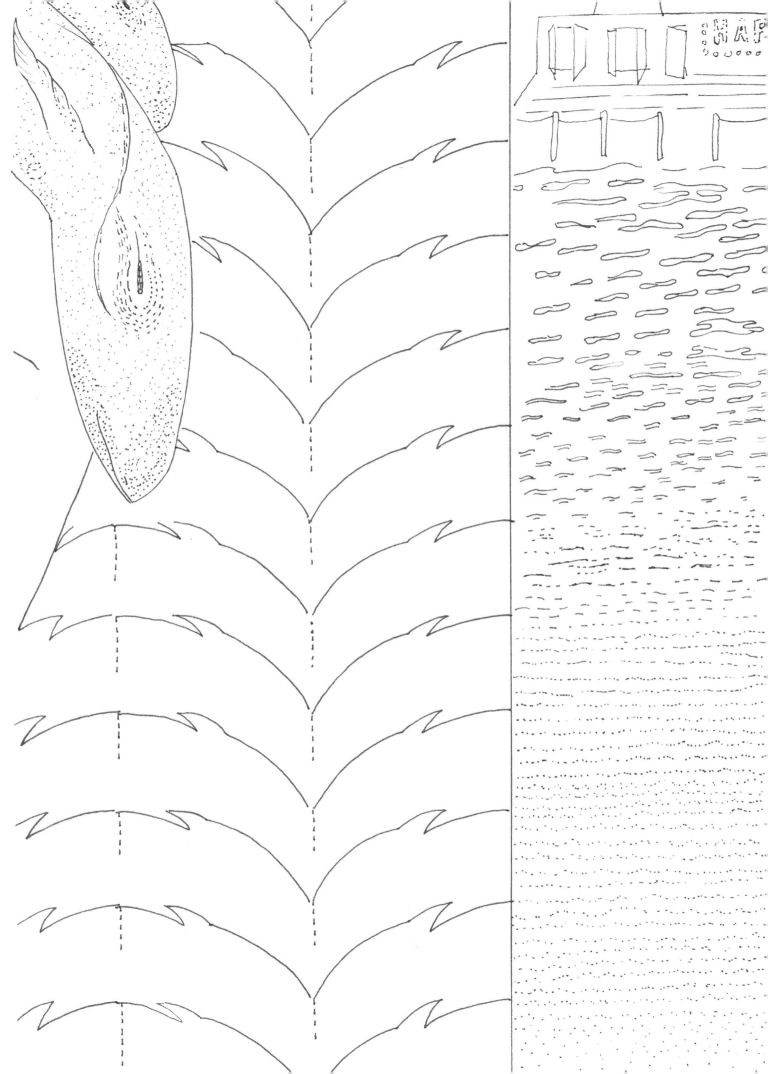

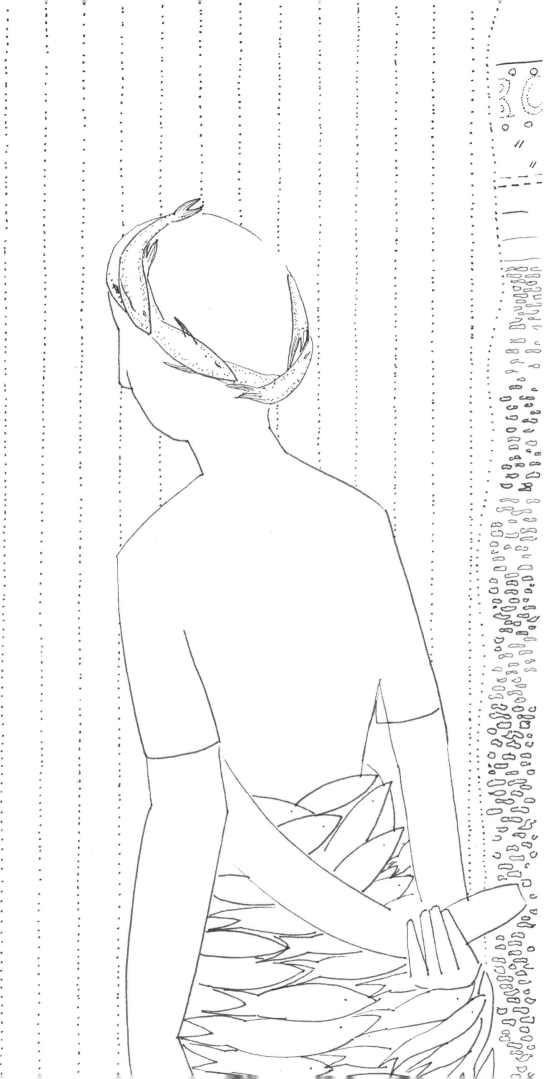

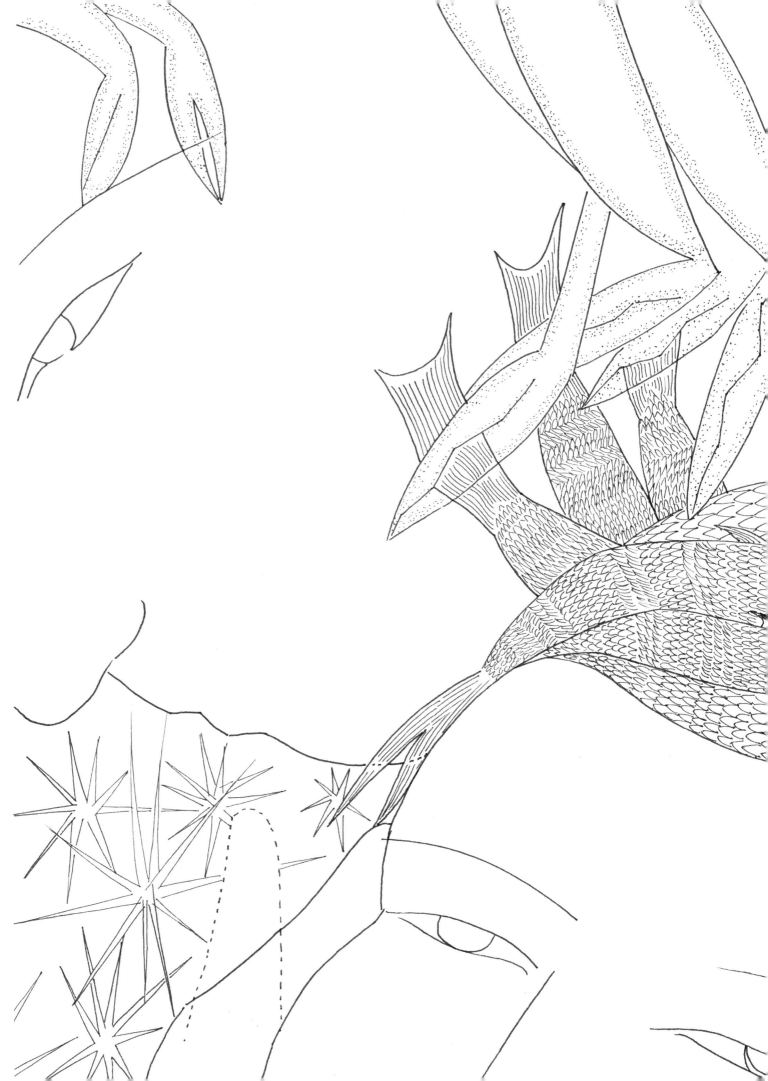

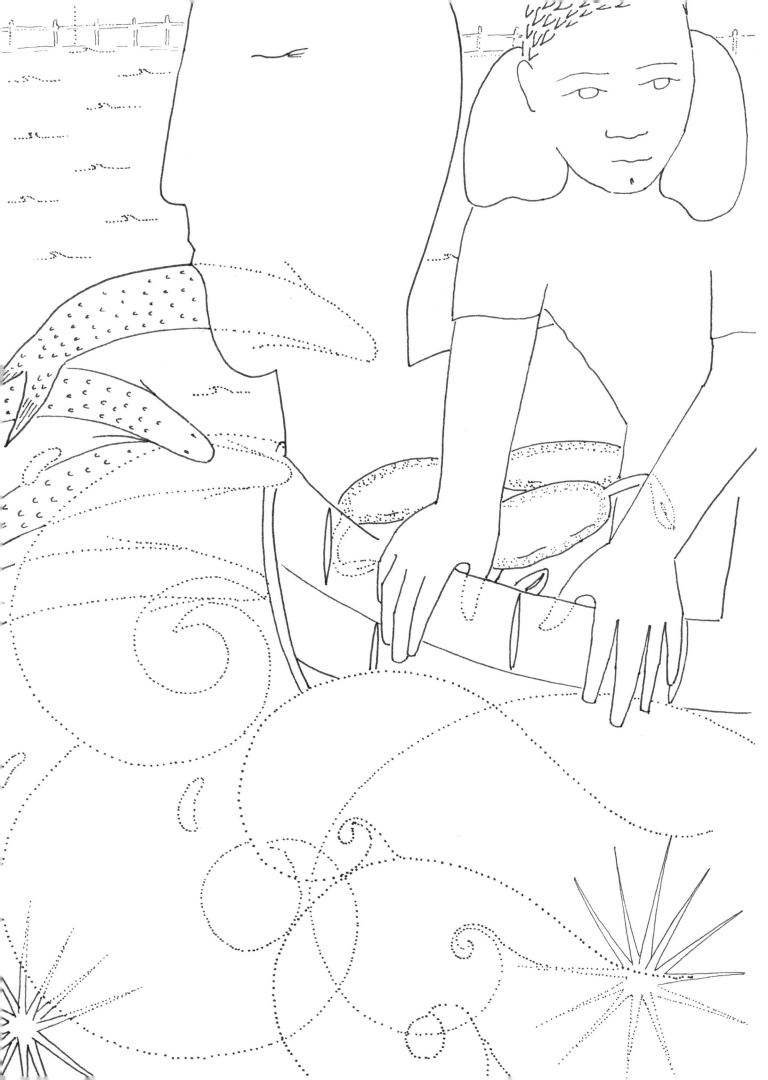

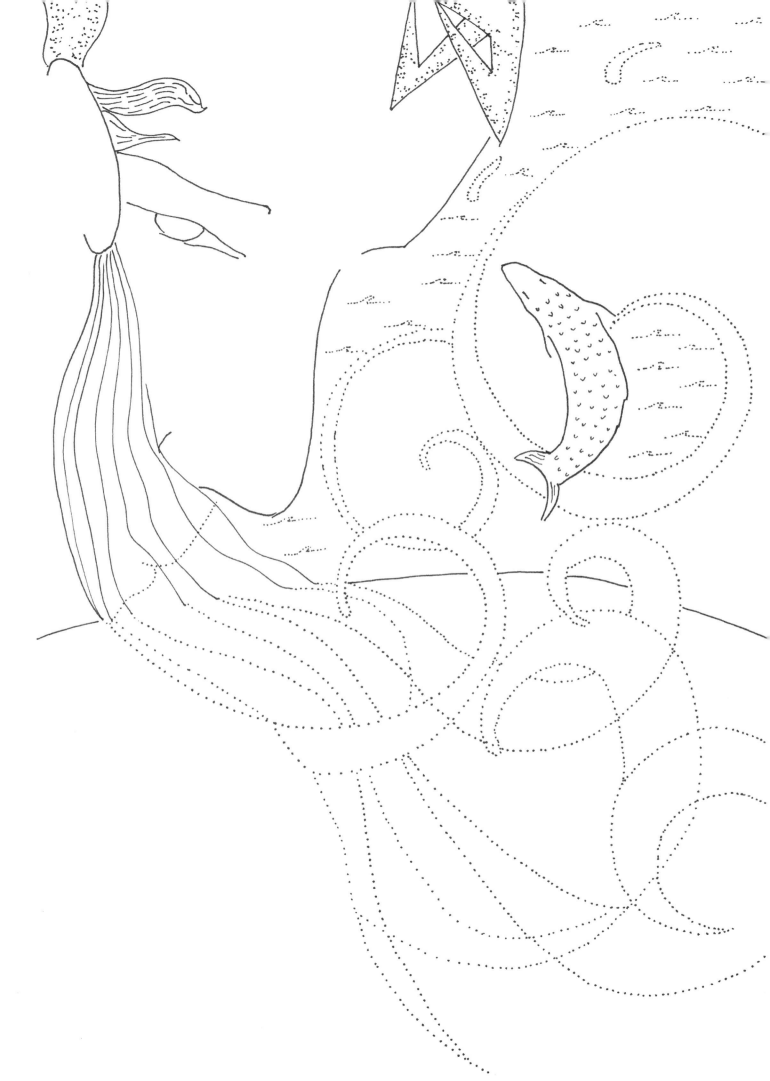

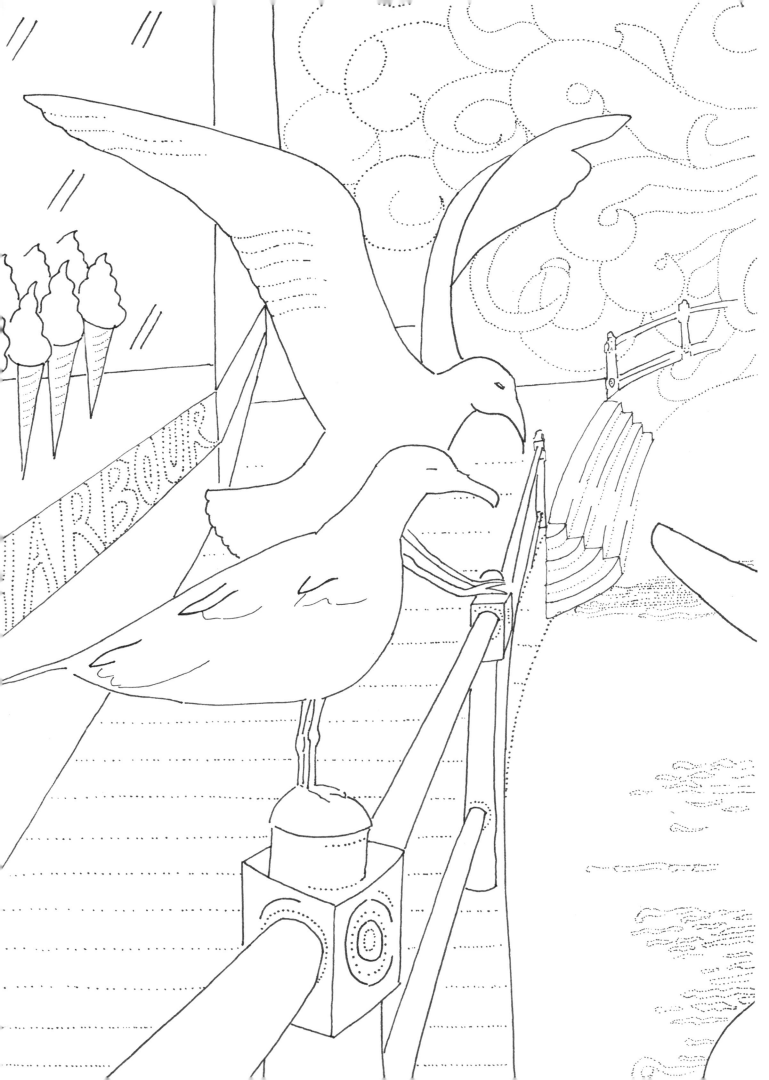

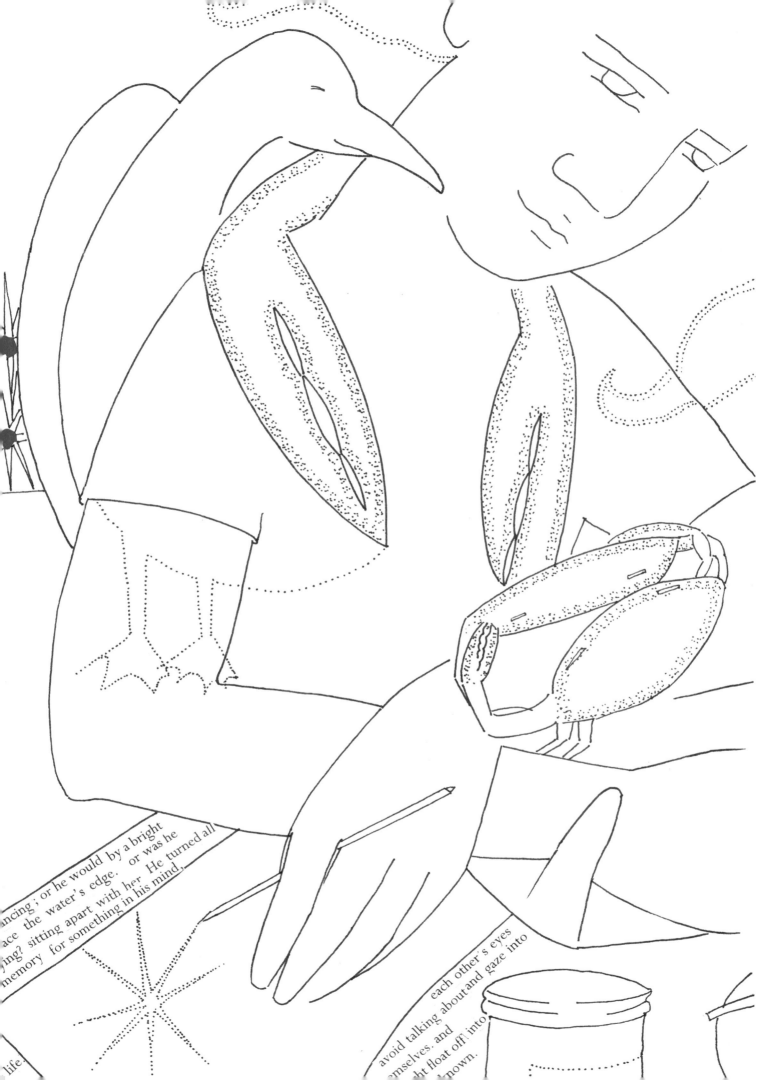

Ocean Swell began on a summer's day two years ago, while working in my studio. I decided to open a sketch book and start drawing. After a few sketches I could see a small story unfold through the main characters, The Boy and The Girl. Initially there was no frame work for the story, instead, each morning was an open page of uncertainty, improvisation and excitement as to where the story may lead. The further the book progressed, the deeper the story developed and now I would like to share this adventure with you.

This book has been supported by crowdfunding website Kickstarter, which seeks to bring creative projects to life through the generosity of many individual sponsors. A short original film was made about Ocean Swell as part of the project, led by Harnake Hunspal with Simon Edwards, Darrall Knight and Poppie Skiöld. Friend and graphic designer Laurie King encouraged the book's creation from sketchbook to publication. Ocean Swell would never have been realised without this help and generous support.

I would like to extend a heartfelt thank you to all of the book's sponsors, some of whom are listed, and, in particular, the Ocean Swell team.